A Pebble for Your Pocket

A Pebble for Your Pocket

THICH NHAT HANH

Parallax Press
Berkeley, California

Parallax Press
P.O. Box 7355
Berkeley, California 94707

Parallax Press is the publishing division of Unified Buddhist Church, Inc.

Printed in the United States of America.

Cover illustration by Philippe Ames.
Illustrations by Nguyen Thi Hop and Nguyen Dong (pp. 4, 8, 13, 32).
Illustrations by Philippe Ames (pp. 2, 17, 21, 22, 28, 35, 41).
Cover and text design by Crowfoot Design.
Author photograph by Simon Chaput.
Back cover photograph by David Rhode.

Library of Congress Cataloging-in-Publication Data
Nhất Hanh, Thích.
A pebble for your pocket / Thich Nhat Hanh.
p. cm.
ISBN 1-888375-05-1
1. Religious Life—Buddhism—Juvenile Literature. I. Title.

BQ5405 .N48 2001
294.3'444'083—dc21

2001036461

1 2 3 4 5 6 7 8 9 10 / 06 05 04 03 02 01

Contents

Precious gems are everywhere in the cosmos
And inside of every one of us.

I want to offer a handful to you, my dear friend.
Yes, this morning, I want to offer a handful to you,
A handful of diamonds that glow from morning to evening.
Each minute of our daily life is a diamond that contains
sky and earth, sunshine and river.

– *Thây*

An Introduction to Thich Nhat Hanh

Thich Nhat Hanh is a Zen Buddhist monk, a peacemaker, a poet, a storywriter, and a beloved teacher. Born in Vietnam, he became a novice monk at the age of sixteen. He is affectionately called Thầy (teacher) by his friends and students.

Thầy came to the United States during the Vietnam War in an effort to put an end to the fighting and bring peace to all countries involved. He now lives in Plum Village, a community of monks, nuns, and laypeople in the south of France. Each year Thầy comes to the United States to give retreats and lectures on the practice of mindfulness.

Old stone buildings, gardens, orchards, fields of sunflowers, and wonderful lotus ponds welcome visitors to Plum Village. People from all over the world come to practice mindful walking, eating, sitting, and breathing meditation. During summer retreats, Thầy devotes the first part of his talks to young people. He also invites children to participate in the many enjoyable, mindful activities offered at Plum Village, including pebble meditation, music, art, drama, and games. From his deep love of children comes *A Pebble for Your Pocket*.

Who Is the Buddha?

Some years ago, I visited a village in India called Uruvela. Two thousand six hundred years ago, a man named Siddhartha lived near that village. Siddhartha is the man who later became known as the Buddha.

The village of Uruvela remains very much the same as it was back then. There are no big buildings, no supermarkets, no freeways. It is very pleasant. The children have not changed either. When Siddhartha lived there, children from that village became his friends and brought him food and simple gifts.

There is a river that runs near the village. It is where Siddhartha used to bathe. A grass called "kusa grass" still grows on the banks of the river. It is the same kind of grass that one of the children gave Siddhartha to use as a cushion to sit on. I walked across the river and I cut some of the kusa grass and brought it home with me.

On the other side of the river, there is a forest. That is where Siddhartha sat in meditation under a tree called the "Bodhi tree." It is under that tree that he became the "Buddha."

A Buddha is anyone who is awake — who is aware of everything that happens inside and around him or her, and who understands and loves deeply. Siddhartha became a fully awakened being — a Buddha. He is the Buddha that we have accepted as

our teacher. He has said that each one of us has a seed of awakening within us and that all of us are future Buddhas.

When he was very young, a student of mine struggled with the question of "Who is the Buddha?" The student's name was Hu, and this is his story.

When Hu was six or seven years old, he asked his father and mother if he could become a monk. Hu loved going to the Buddhist temple. He used to go there with his parents on new moon and full moon days to offer flowers, bananas, mangoes, and all kinds of exotic fruit to the Buddha.

In the temple, Hu was always treated with kindness. When people came to the temple, they seemed more relaxed and friendly. Hu was also aware that the head monk liked him. He would give Hu a banana or a mango every time he came. So that's why Hu loved going to the temple.

One day he said, "Mommy, I want to become a monk and live in the temple." I think he wanted to become a monk because he liked to eat bananas. I don't blame him. In Vietnam, there are several kinds of bananas that are *so* good.

Even though he was young, his father and mother decided to let him go to the temple as a novice. The head monk gave Hu a tiny, brown robe to wear. In his nice new robe, he must have looked like a baby monk.

When he first became a monk, Hu believed that the Buddha loved bananas, mangoes, and tangerines because every time people came to the temple, they brought bananas, mangoes, tangerines,

and other fruit, and placed them in front of the Buddha. In Hu's little head that could only mean that the Buddha loved fruit very much.

One evening, he waited in the temple until all the visitors had gone home. He stood very quietly outside the entrance of the Buddha Hall. He checked to make sure no one else was around. Then he peered into the Buddha Hall. The Buddha statue was as big as a real person. In Hu's very young mind, the statue was the Buddha.

Hu imagined that the Buddha sat very still all day long, and when the hall was empty, he reached out for a banana. Hu waited and watched, hoping to see the Buddha take one of the bananas piled in front of him. He waited for a long time, but he did not see the Buddha pick up a banana. He was baffled. He could not understand why the Buddha did not eat any of the bananas that people brought to him.

Hu did not dare ask the head monk, because he was afraid that the monk would think he was silly. Actually, we often feel like that. We do not dare ask questions because we are afraid we might be called silly. The same was true for Hu. And because he didn't dare ask, he was confused. I think I would have gone to someone and asked. But Hu did not ask anyone.

As he grew older, one day it occurred to him that the Buddha statue was not the Buddha. What an achievement! This realization made him so happy. But then a new question arose. "If the Buddha is not here, then where is he? If the Buddha is not in the temple, where is the Buddha?" Every day he saw people come to the temple and bow to the statue of the Buddha. But where was the Buddha?

In Vietnam, people who practice Pure Land Buddhism believe that the Buddhas stay in the Pure Land, in the direction of the West. One day, Hu overheard someone saying that the Pure Land was the home of the Buddhas. This made Hu believe that the Buddha was in the Pure Land, which made him very unhappy. Why, he wondered, did the Buddha choose to live so far away from people? So this created another question in his mind.

I met Hu when he was fourteen, and he was still wondering about this. I explained to him that the Buddha is not far away from us. I told him that the Buddha is inside each one of us. Being a Buddha is being aware of what is inside of us and around us at every moment. Buddha is the love and understanding that we each carry in our hearts. This made Hu very happy.

When Hu grew up, he became the director of the School of Social Work in Vietnam. He trained young nuns and monks, young men and women, to help people rebuild the villages that had been bombed during the Vietnam War.

Anywhere you see love and understanding, there is the Buddha. Anyone can be a Buddha. Do not imagine that the Buddha is a statue or someone who has a fancy halo around his or her head or wears a yellow robe. A Buddha is a person who is aware of what is going on inside and around him or her and has a lot of understanding and compassion. Whether a Buddha is a man or a woman, young or not so young, a Buddha is always very pleasant and fresh.

The Many Arms of a Bodhisattva

In my experience, there are Buddhas and bodhisattvas present here, in our midst. A bodhisattva (pronouced "bo-dee-sât-vâ") is a compassionate person, someone who cares a lot about helping other beings — someone who vows to become a Buddha.

Statues or pictures of bodhisattvas sometimes show a being with many arms. They are shown this way because a bodhisattva is someone who can do a thousand things at one time. Also, the arms of a bodhisattva can be extremely long and reach very far, helping people in faraway lands. With only two arms, we can only do one or two things at a time. But when you are a bodhisattva, you have many arms, and you can do many things simultaneously. Most of the time, we do not see all the arms of a bodhisattva. One has to be very attentive in order to see the many arms of a bodhisattva.

You may already know someone who is a bodhisattva. It is possible! Your mom, for example, could be a bodhisattva. She does many things at the same time. She needs an arm for cooking. Isn't that true? But at the same time she takes care of you and your brothers and sisters — so she needs a second arm. And then at the same time, she has to run errands. So she needs a third arm. And she has many other things she does that require more arms — she may have a job or she may volunteer at your school. So your mom could be a bodhisattva. The same is true for your dad. Look more deeply at your mother and father and you will see that they have more than two arms.

Do not think that Buddhas and bodhisattvas are beings who exist in heaven. They are right here, all around us. You too can be a bodhisattva if you think of others and do things to bring happiness to them.

If you are awake, if you are present in the moment, here and now, you too are a Buddha. The only difference between you and the Buddha is that he is a full-time Buddha. You are only a part-time Buddha. So you have to live in a way that gives the baby Buddha inside you a chance to grow. Then the baby Buddha will radiate light in all the cells of your body, and you will begin to shine this light.

The Hermit and the Well

I would like to tell you the story of my encounter with the Buddha inside me. When I was a child like you, I lived in North Vietnam, in the province of Thanh Hoa. When I was nine years old, I found a magazine with a black and white drawing of the Buddha on the cover. He was sitting on the grass. He sat beautifully. He looked very peaceful and happy. His face was calm and relaxed, with a little smile. I looked at that picture of the Buddha and it made me feel very peaceful too.

As a little boy, I noticed that the people around me were not usually that calm and peaceful. So when I saw the Buddha, looking so peaceful and happy just sitting on the grass, I wanted to be like him. Even though I did not know anything about the Buddha or his life, when I saw that picture, I felt love for him. After that, I had a strong desire to become someone who could sit as he did, beautifully and peacefully.

One day when I was eleven, my teacher at school announced that we were going to the top of Na Son Mountain to have a picnic. I had never been there before. The teacher told us that at the top of the mountain there lived a hermit. He explained that a hermit was someone who lived alone and practiced day and night to become like the Buddha. How fascinating! I had never seen a hermit before, and I became very excited at the prospect of climbing the mountain and meeting him.

The day before the outing, we prepared food for the picnic. We cooked rice, rolled it into balls, and wrapped the balls in banana leaves. We prepared sesame seeds, peanuts, and salt to dip the rice in. You may never have eaten a rice ball dipped in sesame seeds, peanuts, and salt, but I can tell you it is very delicious. We also boiled water to drink, because it was not safe to drink water straight from the river. Having fresh water to drink is wonderful too.

One hundred and fifty students from my school went on the field trip together. We split up into groups of five. Carrying our picnic with us, we walked for a long time, nearly ten miles, before we reached the foot of the mountain. Then we began our climb.

There were many beautiful trees and rocks along the path. But we did not enjoy them much because we were so anxious to reach the top of the mountain. My friends and I climbed as quickly as we could — we practically ran all the way up the mountain. When I was little, I did not know, as I do now, about the joy of walking meditation — not hurrying, just enjoying each step, the flowers, the trees, the blue sky, and the company of friends.

When my friends and I reached the top, we were exhausted. We had drunk all of our water on the way and did not have even a drop left. Still, I was very eager to find the hermit. We found his hut made of bamboo and straw. Inside, we saw a small bamboo cot and a bamboo altar, but no one was there. What a disappointment! I thought that the hermit must have heard that many boys were coming up the mountain, and since he did not like a lot of talking and noise, he had hidden somewhere.

It was time to have lunch, but I didn't care to eat because I was so tired and disappointed. I thought that maybe if I wandered into the forest I would have a chance to find the hermit. When I was little I had a lot of hope — anything was possible.

So I left my friends and started climbing further up the mountain. As I walked through the forest, I heard the sound of dripping water. You have probably heard it too. It is like the sound of wind chimes or a piano being softly played — very clear and light, like crystal. It was so appealing and peaceful that I started to climb in the direction of the lovely sound, driven also by my great thirst.

It was not long before I came upon a natural well made of stones. I knew that spring water comes up from deep inside the earth. Where the water came up, a natural well made of big rocks of many colors surrounded the spring to form a small pool. The water was high, and so clear that I could see all the way to the bottom. The water looked so fresh and inviting that I knelt down, scooped some in my palms, and began to drink. You cannot imagine my happiness. The water tasted wonderfully sweet. It was so delicious, so refreshing! I felt completely satisfied. I did not have any desire left in me — even the desire to meet the hermit was gone. It is the most wonderful feeling, the feeling of bliss, when you don't desire anything anymore.

Suddenly, it occurred to me that maybe I had met the hermit after all. I began to think that the hermit had magical powers, that he had transformed himself into the well so that I could meet him, and that he cared about me. This made me happy.

I lay down on the ground next to the well and looked up at the sky. I saw the branch of a tree against the blue sky. I was so relaxed, and soon I fell into a deep sleep. I don't know how long I slept, maybe only three or four minutes. When I awoke, I didn't know where I was. When I saw the branch of the tree against the sky and the wonderful well, I remembered everything.

It was time to go back to join the other boys or they might begin to worry about me. I said good-bye to the well and began to walk back down. As I walked out of the forest, a sentence formed in my heart. It was like a poem with only one line: "I have tasted the best water in the world." I will always remember these words.

My friends were glad to see me when I returned. They were laughing and talking loudly, but I had no desire to talk. I was not yet ready to share my experience of the hermit and the well with the other boys. What had happened was something very precious and sacred, and I wanted to keep it to myself. I sat down on the ground and ate my lunch quietly. The rice and the sesame seeds tasted so good. I felt calm and happy and peaceful.

I met my hermit in the form of a well. The image of the well and the sound of dripping water are still alive in me today. You too may have met your hermit, perhaps not as a well but as something else equally marvelous. Perhaps it was a rock, a tree, a star, or a beautiful sunset. The hermit is the Buddha inside of you.

Maybe you haven't met your hermit yet, but if you look deeply, your hermit will be revealed to you. It is inside of you. In fact, all the wonderful things that you are looking for — happiness, peace, and joy — can be found inside of you. You do not need to look anywhere else.

Present Moment Wonderful Moment

"Life is available only in the present moment." This is a simple teaching of the Buddha, but very deep. If someone asked you, "Has the best moment of your life arrived yet?" many of you would probably say that the best moment of your life has not yet come. We all have a tendency to believe that the best moment of our lives has not yet come, but that it will come very soon. But if we continue to live in the same way, waiting for the best moment to arrive, then the best moment will never arrive.

You may believe that your happiness is somewhere else, over there, or in the future, but in fact you can touch your happiness right now. You are alive. You can open your eyes, you can see the sunshine, the beautiful color of the sky, the wonderful vegetation, your friends and relatives around you. This is the best moment of your life!

Enjoying Our Food

Many times when we are eating our food, we are thinking of other things and we don't really know what it is we are eating. When we know what we are eating, it can be so enjoyable. When you sit down to eat, look at your food and know what it is that you are picking up to put into your mouth. If it is a carrot, see that it is a carrot that you are chewing and nothing else. If it is spaghetti, see that it is spaghetti and nothing else — not your anger, not your thoughts about what you are going to do tomorrow.

It only takes half a second to look at a carrot or spaghetti and recognize what you are about to eat. "This is a carrot." "This is spaghetti." It's very important to do this. When you look at the food you are eating and it still does not reveal itself to you, call it by its name: "Carrot," or "Spaghetti." After you call its name, the food will suddenly reveal itself to you.

If you continue to do this, over time you will begin to see the food that you are eating very deeply. Then one day you will see the sunshine, the rain cloud, and all the things and all the people that have come together to make the spaghetti and the carrot in front of you.

When you put food in your mouth and chew it with this kind of awareness, you are chewing something wonderful. When you are truly present with your food, when you eat with all your heart and body, you connect with the whole cosmos. You have the sunshine, the clouds, the earth, time, and space in your mouth. You are in touch with reality, with life.

After eating plums, a child at Plum Village had this to say:

> One day after we ate plums, we examined the pits. I noticed things that I had never seen before, like the various cracks that each pit had. I also noticed that most of them had ridges. In the past, I just threw away the pits. A few of us were able to split them open, and in the middle there is a very small seed. It's really neat.

I had never split open a plum pit before. It helped me to be in the moment. I didn't just throw my pit away and go off looking for something else to do. We also realized that inside each pit there were thousands of plum trees.

TODAY'S DAY

We have all sorts of special days. There is a special day to remember fathers. We call it Father's Day. There is a special day to celebrate our mothers. We call it Mother's Day. There is New Year's Day, Peace Day, and Earth Day. One day a young person visiting Plum Village said, "Why not declare today as 'Today's Day'?" And all the children agreed that we should celebrate today and call it "Today's Day."

On this day, Today's Day, we don't think about yesterday, we don't think about tomorrow, we only think about today. Today's Day is when we live happily in the present moment. When we eat, we know that we are eating. When we drink water, we are aware that it is water we are drinking. When we walk, we really enjoy each step. When we play, we are really present in our play.

Today is a wonderful day. Today is the most wonderful day. That does not mean that yesterday was not wonderful. But yesterday is already gone. It does not mean that tomorrow will not be wonderful. But tomorrow is not yet here. Today is the only day available to us, today, and we can take good care of it. That is why today is so important — the most important day of our lives.

So each morning when you wake up, decide to make that day the most important day. Before you go off to school, sit or lie down, breathe slowly in and out for a few minutes, enjoy your in-breath, enjoy your out-breath, and smile. You are here. You are content. You are peaceful. This is a wonderful way to begin a day.

Try to keep this spirit alive all day. Remember to go back to your breath, remember to look at other people with loving kindness, remember to smile and to be happy with the gift of life. Have a good day today. This is not only a wish. This is a practice.

Return to Your Hermitage

One day I decided to go to the beautiful woods near my hermitage, the place where I live. I took a sandwich and a blanket with me, intending to spend a quiet day by myself in the woods.

That morning, before leaving the hermitage, I had opened all my windows and doors to the sun to dry things out. But in the afternoon the weather changed. The wind began to blow and dark clouds gathered in the sky. Remembering that I had left my hermitage wide open, I decided to return home right away.

When I arrived, I found my hermitage in a very terrible condition. It was cold and dark inside. The wind had blown my papers off the table, and they were scattered all over the floor. It was not at all pleasant.

The first thing I did was to close all the windows and doors. Then I lit the lamp for some light. The third thing I did was to make a fire in the fireplace to warm the place up. When the fire was lit, I picked up the papers from the floor and put them on the table and placed a stone on them.

Then I went back to the fireplace. The fire was burning beautifully. Now there was light, and I was warm. I sat there and listened to the wind howling outside. I imagined the trees tossing in the wind, and I felt very content. It was pleasant sitting next to the fire. I could hear my breathing, my in-breath and my out-breath. I felt very comfortable.

There are moments in our daily lives when we feel miserable, very empty and cold, and we are not happy. It seems that everything is going wrong. You too have probably experienced a feeling like this at some point in your life. Even when we try to make the situation better with things we do or say, nothing seems to work, and we think, "This is not my day." That is exactly how my hermitage was that day.

The best thing to do at a time like this is to go back to yourself, to your hermitage, close all the windows and doors, light a lamp, and make a fire. This means that you have come to a stop. You are no longer busy looking at things, hearing things, or saying things. You have gone back to yourself and become one with your breathing. That is what going back to your hermitage means.

Each of you has a hermitage to go to inside — a place to take refuge and breathe. But this does not mean that you are cutting

yourself off from the world. It means that you are getting more in touch with yourself. Breathing is a good way of doing this. Try it. Just stop where you are and notice your in-breath and your out-breath. With the in-breath, say to yourself, "Breathing in, I am in the present moment." And with the out-breath, say to yourself, "Breathing out, it is a wonderful moment." As you repeat these lines, you can simply use the words "present moment" for the in-breath, and "wonderful moment" for the out-breath. Breathing this way can make you feel really wonderful inside.

Stopping and breathing like this is called mindful breathing or breathing meditation. Breathing mindfully will make your hermitage a lot more comfortable. And when your hermitage inside is comfortable, then your contact with the world outside of you will become more pleasant.

When We Are Angry

When something unpleasant happens, you may become very angry or upset. You may feel like screaming or crying. Maybe your sister or brother does or says something you do not like. It would be better if you could calmly ask your sister or brother, "Why did you do that?" But when you are very angry, usually you just want to scream at the other person or cry.

Because we feel hurt, we want to say or do something to hurt that person back. We think that by saying something cruel back to him or her, we will feel better. But when we say hurtful words back, that person will look for something even more cruel to say. And neither person knows how to stop.

When someone makes you angry, it is better not to respond with words. The first thing to do is to stop and return to your breathing. That's what I do. I say, "Breathing in, I know I am angry. Breathing out, anger is still there." I continue to breathe like this for three or four breaths, and then usually there is a slight change in me, a softening of the anger inside.

We can learn how to act in a way that does not create unhappiness for ourselves or those around us. We can learn to change an unhappy situation into a joyful one. It requires some practice, however. Even though we learn a lot at school, we do not have the opportunity to learn how to be happy or how to suffer less.

Our anger is a part of us. We should not pretend that we are not angry when in fact we are angry. What we need to learn is how to take care of our anger. A good way to take care of our anger is to stop and return to our breathing.

Think of your anger as your little baby brother or sister. No matter what your baby brother or sister has done, you need to treat him or her with tenderness and love, in the same way that a mother comforts her crying baby.

When her baby is crying, a mother takes the baby in her arms and lets him cry, while at the same time she embraces him with love and tenderness. Little by little, the baby becomes calmer, until finally he stops crying altogether. She does not force the baby to stop crying, she envelops him with tenderness and calm.

This is how you should treat your anger, too, with love and tenderness. When you are angry, say:

Breathing in, I know that I am angry.
Breathing out, I am taking good care of my anger.

While you are breathing and saying this, you may still be angry. But you are safe, because you are embracing your anger the way a mother embraces her crying baby. After doing this for a while, your temper will begin to calm down and you will be able to smile at your anger:

Breathing in, I see anger in me.
Breathing out, I smile at my anger.

When we take care of our anger like this, we are being "mindful." Mindfulness acts just like the rays of the sun. Without any effort, the sun shines on everything and everything changes because of it. When we expose our anger to the light of mindfulness, it will change, too, like a flower opening to the sun.

A Pebble for Your Pocket

Sometimes when we become angry during the day, it is difficult to remember to stop and breathe. I know a good way for you to remember to stop and breathe when you are angry or upset. First, go for a walk and find a pebble that you like. Then, go sit near the Buddha, if there is one in your house, or outside under a special tree or on a special rock, or go to your room. With the pebble in your hand, say:

> Dear Buddha,
> Here is my pebble. I am going to practice with it when things go wrong in my day. Whenever I am angry or upset, I will take the pebble in my hand and breathe deeply. I will do this until I calm down.

Now put your pebble in your pocket and take it with you wherever you go. When something happens during the day that makes you unhappy, put your hand in your pocket, take hold of the pebble, breathe deeply, and say to yourself, "Breathing in, I know I am angry. Breathing out, I am taking good care of my anger." Do this until you feel a lot better and can smile to your anger.

Walking Meditation

Another wonderful way to calm down when we are upset is by walking. As we walk, we pay attention to each step we take. We notice how each foot touches the ground. The Earth is our mother. When we are away from Mother Nature, we get sick. Each step we take allows us to touch our mother, so that we can be well again. A lot of harm has been done to Mother Earth, so now it is time to kiss the Earth with our feet, with our love.

While you are walking, smile — be in the here and the now. By doing so, you transform the place where you are walking into paradise. Walk slowly. Don't rush. Each step brings you to the best moment of your life, the present moment.

If you say the following gatha (poem) to yourself while you walk, your walk will be even more enjoyable:

Breathing in, I know I am breathing in.
Breathing out, I know I am breathing out.

As my in-breath grows deep,
My out-breath grows slow.

Breathing in, I calm my body,
Breathing out, I feel at ease.

Breathing in, I smile,
Breathing out, I release.

Dwelling in the present moment,
I know this is a wonderful moment.

As you continue walking and breathing, you can shorten the gatha to: in/out, deep/slow, calm/ease, smile/release, present moment/wonderful moment.

During your walk, stop to observe the beautiful things around you, above you, and below you. Continue to breathe in and out, in order to get in touch with these wonderful things. The moment you stop being aware of your breathing, the beautiful things may vanish, and thinking and worrying may settle in your mind again.

Just allow yourself to be! Allow yourself to enjoy being in the present moment. The Earth is so beautiful. Enjoy the planet Earth. You are beautiful too, you are a marvel like the Earth. To walk like this is called walking meditation.

Remember that while you are walking, you are not going anywhere, yet every step helps you to arrive. To arrive where? To arrive in the present moment — to arrive in the here and now. You don't need anything else to be happy.

Some of the children at Plum Village expressed it this way:

> GAIA: Walking meditation is so you notice everything around you. You listen to your breath. If you don't ever walk mindfully, your whole life can pass by without you noticing it. Think what a pity it would be if you passed through your life thinking only about what is going to happen next and never noticed anything else, never knew what the world was like at all. That would be pretty sad.

TY: It involves a lot of patience to be mindful. When you are mindful, your mind is full of the things around you, full of your breathing, feeling the rocks under your feet, and that's mindfulness. You are in the present moment, you are aware of what you are doing. You know that you are walking, and that you are walking with Thây. Your mind can't be somewhere else, thinking about eating dinner. It has to be right where you are. And that's walking meditation.

ANOTHER CHILD SAID: I think that what is special about walking meditation is that you can notice everything around you. You take everything in, like the blue sky. We can be in touch with many, many wonderful things.

The Lotus Pond

In Plum Village, where I live in France, there is a beautiful lotus pond. Maybe one day you will come to Plum Village and you can see it. In the summer the pond is covered with hundreds of beautiful lotus blossoms. What is amazing is that all the lotus plants in the pond come from a single tiny seed. I will tell you how to grow a lotus pond.

Lotus seeds have to be planted in wet soil. They do not grow well in dry soil. But there is a trick to planting a lotus seed. If you just put the seed into the mud, it will not sprout, even if you wait three weeks, five weeks, or ten weeks. But it will not die, either. There are lotus seeds more than one thousand years old that when planted properly have grown into lotus plants.

The lotus seed does not sprout if you just place it in the mud because the lotus seed needs some help to sprout. The lotus seed is a kernel with very hard skin covering it. In order to sprout, water needs to penetrate into the lotus seed through the hard skin. That is the trick. You need to make a little hole in the seed so that the water can get in.

You can pierce the outer skin by cutting into it with a knife or by rubbing it against a rock. This will give water a chance to penetrate into the seed. Now if you place it in the water or in the mud, in about four or five days the tiny seed will sprout and become a tiny lotus plant.

At first a few small lotus leaves will appear. Soon they will grow bigger. You can keep a little lotus plant in your yard during the spring, summer, or autumn. But when it is cold, you have to bring it inside, where it will continue to grow.

In the spring you can bring it out again and put it in a larger container, and the lotus plant will grow even bigger. In one year you will have a few lotus flowers, and in three years you will have a lotus pond as big as the one in Plum Village.

So you see, a huge lotus pond truly is contained within one tiny seed. This tiny seed contains all the ancestors of the lotus plant — it contains their fragrance and beauty, and all their characteristics. As this seed sprouts and begins to grow, it offers all these gifts to the world.

Each of you is a wonderful seed like the lotus seed. You look a little bigger than a lotus seed, but you are a seed nonetheless. In you there is understanding and love and many, many different talents. From our ancestors we receive wonderful seeds. Our ability to play music or paint, to run fast or do math, to make things with our hands or dance are all seeds we receive from our ancestors. We also inherit seeds that are not so nice, like the seeds of fear and anger. These seeds of fear and anger can make us very unhappy and often we don't know what to do.

Some time ago, a twelve-year-old Swiss boy and his sister started coming regularly to Plum Village. The boy had a problem with his father. He was very angry at his father because his father did not speak kindly to him. Whenever the boy fell down or hurt himself, instead of helping and comforting him, his father got angry at him. He would say, "You're stupid! Why did you do such a thing?"

The boy of course wanted his father to comfort him with kind words when he was in pain. He could not understand why his father treated him this way, and he vowed that he would never act like his father when he grew up. If he had a son, he would help him up and comfort him should he fall and hurt himself.

One day, this boy was watching his sister play on a hammock with another girl. They were swinging back and forth. Suddenly, the hammock turned over and both girls fell to the ground. His sister cut her forehead. When the boy saw his sister bleeding, he became furious. He was about to shout at her, "You're stupid! Why did you hurt yourself like that?" But because he knew how to practice, he caught himself, and went back to his breathing. Seeing that his sister was all right, he decided to do walking meditation.

During his walking meditation, he discovered something wonderful. He saw that he was exactly like his father. He had the same kind of energy that pushed him to say unkind words. When your loved ones are suffering, you should be loving, tender, and helpful, and not shout at them out of anger. He saw that he was about to behave exactly like his father. That was his insight. Imagine a twelve-year-old boy practicing like that. He realized he was the continuation of his father and had the same kind of energy, the same negative seeds.

Continuing to walk mindfully, he discovered that he could not transform his anger without practice, and that if he did not practice, he would transmit the same energy of anger to his children. I think it is remarkable for a twelve-year-old boy to succeed like this in meditation. He gained these two insights in less than fifteen minutes of walking meditation.

His third and final insight was that when he returned home he would discuss his discoveries with his father. He decided to ask his father to practice with him so that both of them could transform their energy. With this third insight, his anger at his father vanished because he understood that his father was also a victim. His father might have received this energy from his own father. So you see, the practice of looking deeply to gain understanding and freedom from your anger is very important.

THE PRECIOUS GEM

In Buddhism, there is an image of the world that is very wonderful. The image shows a world full of bright, shiny jewels. This world is called the Dharmakaya (pronounced "Dar-ma-ky-ya"). The Dharmakaya is not separate from the world we see everyday. When we look closely, we will discover that our everyday world is full of wonderful treasures. Long ago, Buddha told a story to remind us that these wonderful treasures are always there for us, if only we are able to see them.

Once there was a rich man who had a very lazy son. The young man didn't know how to do anything except spend his father's money. Because he was the son of a rich man, he never learned a trade and did not know how to make a living.

The father was afraid that after he died, his son would sell everything in the house and become a pauper. Although he tried very hard to change his son, in the end the father realized that this would not happen in his lifetime.

Yet, the father loved his son very much and he could not stop worrying about him. Then one evening after much thought, he had an idea. The next morning, he went to his tailor and asked him to make a warm jacket. When the jacket was finished, the old man took it home and wore it everyday until it began to look used.

One day, he called his son to him and said, "My son, when I die you will inherit everything that I have. I hope that you will manage your inheritance well. If, however, you decide to sell my belongings, I ask just one thing." Picking up his jacket, he said, "I ask that you keep this jacket and wear it all the time. This will be enough to make me happy."

The son looked at his father's worn jacket. This he could easily do.

"Don't worry, Father, I promise I will not sell it."

Soon after that the father died, and the young man inherited all his wealth. And just as his father had anticipated, the son sold all his belongings. He kept his promise, however, and did not sell the jacket.

It was not long before the son had spent all the money received from selling his father's valuables. And as his father had feared, his son became very poor. One by one, his friends abandoned him. And since he did not know how to make a living for himself, he soon became homeless.

Without a home or friends, the son began to wander from place to place. Many nights he had to sleep outside under a tree without dinner. But he still had his father's jacket to keep him warm.

Many years passed and the son still wandered from place to place without a roof over his head. Then one day, while he was lying on the ground, he felt something hard under his body. At first he thought it was a stone on the ground beneath him. But when he looked, there was no stone.

Determined to find out what the hard thing was, he checked inside the pockets of the jacket he was wearing, but there was nothing. He became more curious, and he searched the entire jacket. Suddenly he felt something inside the lining of the threadbare jacket. He cut into the lining, and, to his surprise, out dropped a gem. His father had put a precious gem in the lining of the jacket!

After so many years of thinking that he was poor, the son realized that he was rich. But now he had learned his lesson. He would not squander his inheritance this time. He bought a house and started a business. He began to earn his living. He was overjoyed! Grateful that he had a second chance, he was happy to share his wealth with others.

After telling this story, the Buddha said that we are all like the son. We too have inherited great wealth but like the son, we don't know it, and we behave as if we were poor. We have a treasure of enlightenment, of understanding, of love, and of joy inside us. And if we know how to rediscover them and allow them to manifest, we shall be extremely happy. There are many chances for us to be happy. But we keep thinking that we are only a destitute son or daughter.

So it is time to go back to receive your inheritance. Being mindful will help you claim it. With mindfulness you will see that you have many gems in the lining of your jacket. You need only to look up in order to see the blue sky. You need only to breathe in and out to see that today is beautiful and worth living. You need only to breathe in and out to see that those you love are still alive around you, and you can be very, very happy.

This is a poem I wrote after I read the Buddha's story about the rich man and his son:

Precious gems are everywhere in the cosmos
And inside of every one of us.

I want to offer a handful to you, my dear friend.
Yes, this morning, I want to offer a handful to you,
A handful of diamonds that glow from morning to evening.
Each minute of our daily life is a diamond that contains
sky and earth, sunshine and river.

We only need to breathe gently for the miracle to be revealed:
Birds singing, flowers blooming.

Here is the blue sky, here is the white cloud floating,
your lovely look, your beautiful smile.
All these are contained in one jewel.

You who are the richest person on Earth and behave
like a destitute son,
Please come back to your heritage.

Let us offer each other happiness and learn to
Dwell in the present moment.
Let us cherish life in our two arms
And let go of our forgetfulness and despair.

Ways to Practice

Eating an Orange

When you look deeply at an orange, you realize that an orange — or any fruit — is nothing less than a miracle. Try it. Take an orange and hold it in your palm. Breathe in and out slowly, and look at it as if you were seeing it for the first time.

When you look at it deeply, you will be able to see many wonderful things — the sun shining and the rain falling on the orange tree, the orange blossoms, the tiny fruit appearing on the branch, the color of the fruit changing from green to yellow, and then the full-grown orange. Now slowly begin to peel it. Smell the wonderful scent of the orange peel. Break off a section of the orange and put it into your mouth. Taste its wonderful juice.

The orange tree has taken three, four or six months to make such an orange for you. It is a miracle. Now the orange is ready and it says, "I am here for you." But if you are not present, you will not hear it. When you are not looking at the orange in the present moment, then the orange is not present either.

Being fully present while eating an orange, an ice cream cone, or any other food is a delightful experience.

Tree-Hugging

When you touch a tree, you receive something beautiful and refreshing back. Trees are wonderful! They are also solid, even in a storm. We can learn a lot from trees.

Find a tree that is especially beautiful to you — perhaps it's an apple tree, an oak tree, or a pine tree. If you stop and touch a tree deeply, you will feel its wonderful qualities. Breathing deeply will help you touch the tree deeply. Breathe in, touch the tree, then breathe out. Do this three times. Touching the tree in this way will make you feel refreshed and happy.

Then, if you like, you can hug the tree. Tree-hugging is a wonderful practice. When you hug a tree, a tree never refuses. You can rely on a tree. It is dependable. Every time you want to see it, every time you need its shade, it is there for you.

In my home in Plum Village, I planted three cedar trees. I planted them about thirty years ago, and now they are very big and beautiful, and very refreshing. While I am doing walking meditation, I usually stop in front of one of the trees. I bow to it. It makes me feel happy. I touch the bark with my cheek. I smell the tree. I look up at the beautiful leaves. I feel the strength and freshness of the tree. I breathe in and out deeply. It's very pleasant, and sometimes I stay for a long time, just enjoying the lovely tree.

Touching the Earth

In Plum Village we do a practice called "Touching the Earth" every day. It helps us in many ways. You too could be helped by doing this practice. When you feel restless or lack confidence in yourself, or when you feel angry or unhappy, you can kneel down and touch the Earth deeply with your hand. Touch the Earth as if it were your favorite thing or your best friend.

The Earth has been there for a long time. She is mother to all of us. She knows everything. The Buddha asked the Earth to be his witness by touching her with his hand when he had some doubt and fear before his awakening. The Earth appeared to him as a beautiful mother. In her arms she carried flowers and fruit, birds and butterflies, and many different animals, and offered them to the Buddha. The Buddha's doubts and fears instantly disappeared.

Whenever you feel unhappy, come to the Earth and ask for her help. Touch her deeply, the way the Buddha did. Suddenly, you too, will see the Earth with all her flowers and fruit, trees and birds, animals, and all the living beings that she has produced. All these things she offers to you.

You have more opportunities to be happy than you ever thought. The Earth shows her love to you and her patience. The Earth is very patient. She sees you suffer, she helps you, she protects you. When we die, she takes us back into her arms.

With the Earth you are very safe. She is always there, in all her wonderful expressions like tress, flowers, butterflies, and sunshine. Whenever you are tired or unhappy, Touching the Earth is a very good practice to heal you and restore your joy.

Arranging Flowers

We arrange flowers because we want life to be beautiful. When we know how to arrange flowers, then we know how to be with ourselves and people around us, because we are all flowers. As we arrange flowers, we arrange ourselves.

To make a flower arrangement, first you need to find a flower. Perhaps there is a garden or a field where you can pick a flower. When you pick a flower, you can show your appreciation for its presence, for its beauty, by saying "thank you" and smiling to it. Do this before picking it and also after picking it. Put it in a container of fresh water immediately, so that it will be nourished right away.

You might think that you need many flowers to make a flower arrangement. But in fact, even without flowers, you can make beautiful arrangements. All you need is a branch from the ground, dry leaves, a rock, a feather, or some sand. Thank them as you thanked the flower, and sit down and start arranging them.

Arrange the things you have chosen in such a way that there is peace and harmony among them. If you breathe and smile while you are arranging them, the feeling of peace inside of you and inside the arrangement grows. But if you just throw the various items together without care, when you step back and look, you won't see peace because the different pieces are fighting each other.

When you arrange flowers, you also arrange the space in between and around the flowers and other items. Space between flowers creates a sense of freedom in us and in the hearts of people looking at the arrangement.

Flower arranging takes time. There is no need to hurry. Rushing defeats your purpose. Allow yourself enough time so that you stay very present during the process. That way, your flower arranging will create beauty and peace, and will be enjoyable to you and everyone else.

After you have finished your flower arrangement, you might want to give it a name and say it out loud. You can draw a picture of your creation and write its name. You can send your drawing to me in Plum Village, if you like.

I Have Arrived

Parallax Press publishes books and tapes on mindfulness practices and Buddhism. For a copy of our free catalog, please write to:

Parallax Press
P.O. Box 7355
Berkeley, California 94707
www.parallax.org

Thich Nhat Hanh has retreat communities in southwestern France (Plum Village), Vermont (Green Mountain Dharma Center), and California (Deer Park Monastery), where monks, nuns, laymen, and laywomen practice the art of mindful living.

Families and children are especially welcome at the Plum Village Summer Opening. For information, please visit www.plumvillage.org or write to:

Plum Village
13 Martineau,
33580 Dieulivol
France

Green Mountain Dharma Center
P.O. Box 182
Hartland Four Corners, VT 05049

Deer Park Monastery
2499 Melru Lane
Escondido, CA 92026